RAVEN
CHILD
and
THE SNOW WITCH

Written by
LINDA SUNDERLAND

Illustrated by
DANIEL EGNÉUS

t
templar publishing

$\mathcal{I}$f you walked for one hundred nights and one hundred days across the frozen Lonesome Lakes, over the Shimmery Mountains . . .

. . . and through
the Forest of a
Thousand Eyes . . .

. . . you would come at last to the Snow Garden.
Here, safe from the dangers of the icy wilderness,
lived little Anya with her mother and father.

Every day, Anya swayed among the branches of the tall fir trees where the ravens nested. She spoke their language, learning of their journeys over the ice fields and endless forests Out There. They wove her a dress of feathers that fluttered in the wind.

On this particular day, the first of spring, the ravens set off with Anya's mother to the glacier, where she went every year to collect blue gentian flowers to plant in the Snow Garden. They were Anya's special lucky flower and they glowed in the dark like sapphires.

Father clanged and banged in his workshop
as usual. For many years he had been building
strange contraptions that he hoped one day
would give him the power to fly like a bird.
Anya stayed to help him for a while, then
went outside.

As she waited for her mother to return,
she fell asleep and dreamed.

In her dream, Anya saw the glacier's jagged form, and she saw her mother's face as if through frosted glass. Then she heard these haunting words: *The Snow Witch has taken me prisoner and I do not know if I will ever see you again. Always remember I love you, Anya.*

Anya awoke in fear and ran to Father's workshop. She told him about her dream. He put down his tools and hugged her tightly. His eyes were troubled and as he looked out across the garden, he saw a ragged black shape struggling towards them. It was a raven, his broken wing trailing in the snow.

The raven had a terrible story to tell.

*W*e *flew to the mountains to feed on berries; we flew high enough to see the curve of the earth, low enough to see salmon leaping up the waterfalls. We circled the glacier, listening to its groans and creaks.*

At the glacier's edge, we watched your mother picking flowers, Anya. Then, the glacier seemed to breathe, sucking her into its icy depths. I saw my friends beat their wings in panic as they too were swallowed up. I was nearly caught, but as the ice closed around my wing, I managed to drag myself free.

$\mathcal{A}$nya looked at her father in horror.

'Mother!' she cried, tears streaming down her face. 'We must go to her!'

'It is not safe to leave now,' her father told her gently. 'Better to wait until morning.'

Anya cradled the raven in her arms and carried him into the warm house.

She made a splint for his wing and tucked him up in front of the fire.

'Poor Broken Wing,' she whispered as she stroked his wounded body. Anya slept fitfully that night, thinking of her mother trapped in that icy place far away from everything she loved.

The next morning Father was preparing for the journey. Anya begged to go with him. 'It will be dangerous,' he told her. 'Are you not afraid?'

'Yes, very afraid, Father, but more afraid of never seeing Mother again.'

Father hugged her close. 'If I can be half as brave as you are, little Anya, together we will not fail.'

Anya packed food into a small basket lined with her lucky gentians, and with Broken Wing gripping her shoulder, they set off.

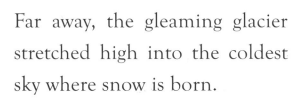

Far away, the gleaming glacier
stretched high into the coldest
sky where snow is born.

*B*efore long, there was snow in the bitter wind. They struggled onwards into a blizzard until it was impossible to go any further. Father lit a fire and as Anya grew sleepy she thought she could hear her mother calling to her through the darkness.

She was woken suddenly by the cold howling of wolves, which filled the air with fear. Broken Wing cawed his terrible cry and flexed his sharp claws as the pack came closer.

Then a frightened creature burst through the trees, and crouched, trembling, by the fire. There was blood on its fur. The snarling wolves were angry to be cheated of their meal, but Father and Anya waved burning brands at them. The wolves backed away, their eyes gleaming in the depths of the forest.

The hunted creature shook its silvery fur and sniffed
the air with its pointy nose; it was an Arctic fox, ghost
of the snow. Anya could see that some of his tail was
missing. He licked Anya's hand and let her tend his
wound. 'Poor Half Tail,' she said, stroking his head.

It was time to struggle on. They set off with
Half Tail into the storm, sheltering each other
from hailstones and comforting each other in
the lightning that stabbed the darkening sky.

*T*hey trudged many miles, until at last they saw lights from a village. As they approached, the air filled with tears, and the villagers told them of the beautiful woman who had enchanted their children and stolen them away the day before.

Half Tail raised his nose and sniffed the air.
He began to circle the crowd. Then his fur
stood on end and he ran towards the hill.
Father began to gather the villagers together
to follow Half Tail, but Anya was impatient.

With Broken Wing cawing his great cry, Anya pushed on into the snow, ignoring her father's calls that grew fainter and fainter, while her mother's words of love from the dream grew louder in her head.

*H*ours later, exhausted and afraid, Anya reached the glacier's splintered edge, where she found broken gentians strewn about and a drift of raven feathers. She knew she had come to the right place. She gathered her mother's flowers and wept as she put them with her own. Then with Broken Wing nuzzling his beak into her hair to give her comfort, she found a narrow opening in the ice and slipped inside.

Anya gasped as the glacier sealed itself behind her. As she scattered the luminous flowers to make a path of light through the darkness, Anya saw with a shock the ravens and the village children rigid inside great blocks of ice.

Then, through the silence came a sound that filled her with joy and hope. It was a song that her mother had sung to her many times as a baby to comfort her when she was sad. Anya squeezed herself between the icy walls and entered a great cave.

And she knew that this was where she would face her deepest fears. A tall, still figure spoke from the shadows in a voice as cold as a winter wind. 'Welcome, foolish Anya, to my frozen world where ice grows its crystals in the marrow of your bones.' The Snow Witch stepped into the light and Anya's heart jumped in fear, though she spoke in a voice as strong as steel.

'I am not afraid of you, Snow Witch. You have stolen someone I love and I mean to take her back with me.'

The Snow Witch laughed. 'And how do you plan to do that, when I have the power to bring the world to a stop with one blast of my icy breath?'

*A*nya had no answer. She felt the terrible force of this creature. But her heart glowed warm and strong within her. She was suddenly aware of a change in the air.

'Listen,' she said. There was a drip-dripping and a trickling of water. The ice was melting. The children stretched their cramped bodies and the ravens burst from their ice prisons, free at last. Anya could feel her mother close by.

'This is my power,' said Anya. 'I have brought the warmth of my love into your cold kingdom, and you cannot fight it.'

The Snow Witch shrieked as her world began to melt and she felt her power failing. The ravens caught hold of her hair and pulled her upwards, crashing through the glacier like black fireworks. She shattered into a thousand jagged crystals that sank into the depths of the ocean.

Anya ran to her mother, and together, their hearts bursting with happiness, they led the children along the gentian path to safety. As they came out into the light, Father and the villagers rushed to meet them.

Father held Anya and her mother as if he would never let them go. Broken Wing cawed, and Half Tail wagged his ragged tail, yelping with delight.

It was late when the tired but happy family reached the safety of the Snow Garden. Before long, the fire blazed, and a meal was cooked. Then Anya and her mother were overcome with sleep.

But Father disappeared into his workshop and toiled all night long. The next morning, he had a surprise for his brave little Anya.

As he placed a magical winged crown on her head, Anya felt her body lift and her bones become like a bird's. Her feathered dress flickered into life and she rose up into the sky.

She was flying, flying with the ravens.